Henbit and the Roly Poly
A Frendibles Story

Written and Illustrated
by Marty Donnellan

Henbit and the Roly Poly
A Frendibles Story

Written and Illustrated by
Marty Donnellan

ISBN-13: 978-0692205174

ISBN-10: 0692205179

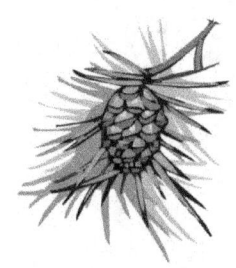

Pine Cone Press

www.thefrendiblesplace.com

Other Books by Marty Donnellan

Fiction

Henbit and Her Sisters

(Book One of The Forest of the Frendibles)

Tegera

(Book Two of The Forest of the Frendibles)

Henbit and Maypop

Non-Fiction

Cloth Characters: A Book of Doll Patterns and Ideas

Teach Someone to Roller Skate – Even Yourself!

Frendibles are small creatures who live in the woods, meadows and thickets of the southern United States. No bigger than baking potatoes, they live in abandoned foxholes, mole burrows or the holes left by the roots of fallen pines. They have many friends, a few enemies, and lots of adventures!

CHAPTER 1

Sweetflag burst into Henbit's dim underground bedroom.

"Come with me, it's a beautiful day outside!" the young frendible cried, yanking at her oldest sister's sleeve.

Henbit swatted at Sweetflag from her rocking chair. "Stop pulling at me," she grumbled. "Can't you see I'm mending?"

"But the dogwoods have turned the prettiest shade of red! Besides, you're not mending, you're sitting there staring."

Henbit looked startled. "Well, I was thinking about mending." She glared at the large basket of clothes by her bed. "Just look at that pile."

"But I've got something to show you," Sweetflag said, looking sad.

"Don't you ever trim those bangs?" Henbit interrupted. "I can hardly see your eyes."

"Come with me, it's a beautiful day outside!"

"I'll cut them tonight if you'll come outside," Sweetflag promised.

"And do what, swing from the vines like a squirrel? Just look at your knees, Flag, they're one big scab. I'd be worried about infections if I were you. And why are you still wearing shorts in the middle of fall? Head colds can lead to pneumonia, you know."

"All my long pants are in the basket," Sweetflag said with a shrug.

Henbit shook her finger. "It's that tree climbing obsession of yours," she declared. "It's ruining your life. You don't bathe, your clothes are in tatters and you don't lift a finger to help out. Well, somebody's got to show some responsibility around here. Somebody's got to set an example."

"Aw, Henbit, you're so boring. Come outside and have some fun for a change. There's something I want you to see."

Henbit was about to object that somebody had to be boring or nothing would ever get done, when she noticed her other sister Cloudberry posing in the doorway. Cloudberry had paused, hoping for a compliment on her gauzy, hand embroidered blouse and her twirly, tiered skirt.

Cloudberry paused, hoping for a compliment...

"Cloudberry, make her leave me alone," Henbit ordered instead.

Cloudberry sighed as her arms dropped. "Flag, you're not goading Henbit again, are you?"

"Goading, of course I'm not goading," Sweetflag said. "I'm just trying to show her something neat outside and she won't cooperate. That's a pretty blouse, Cloudy," she added.

"Thanks, I designed it myself. It goes nicely with my wispy blond hair, don't you think?" Cloudberry gave her skirt an extra twirl as Henbit rolled her eyes. "Hennie, you really should come outside," she coaxed. "It's a glorious day."

"But somebody's got to set an example," Henbit repeated. She got up and plucked a pair of Sweetflag's pants from the basket. "See? She was supposed to wash these first."

Sweetflag shrugged again. "I forgot."

"Not to change the subject, Hennie," Cloudberry said, "but we think you stay holed up inside here entirely too much – don't we, Flag? You look so puffy and pale... Frendibles are meant to spend their days outside, among the pines, in the thicket. Don't you want to look healthy, and, and radiant?" Without intending to, Cloudberry touched her own pink face, and blushed.

Henbit gave a sigh that sounded more like a honk. "If I go outside for five minutes, will you two promise to leave me alone?"

CHAPTER 2

Her sisters nodded eagerly. Muttering under her breath, Henbit straightened her thick stockings under her dark tweed suit. She put on her sensible black shoes and adjusted her dark straw hat which was already on her head. She began to look around.

"You really don't need your purse and medical bag, too," Cloudberry said gently. "We're just going out for a little air."

Still protesting, Henbit followed her sisters up the dim tunnel and into the cool, golden afternoon. Her gusting, unhappy sighs turned into a gasp of pleasure. The dogwoods were crimson and fiery against the brown and olive pines. The sky beyond them was a deep and perfect blue. Even the holly bushes sported festive red berries.

"It is a pretty day," Henbit admitted, feeling her shoulders relax. "What did you want to show me, Flag?"

Sweetflag peered at her sister from behind un-trimmed bangs. "Remember last week when you said you weren't afraid of anything?"

Henbit felt her shoulders tense up again. "So?"

Sweetflag pointed to a rock on the ground. "So, look what's on this rock. A roly poly."

Henbit turned to Cloudberry and exploded, "You see how she does me?"

"Why, Flag, that's not very sisterly." Cloudberry frowned. "You know Henbit is terrified of roly polies."

Henbit's hands flew to her hips. "I am not!" she retorted.

"Yes, you are," Sweetflag said. "And if you'll pick this one up, I'll do all the dishes for a week."

"Ha!" Henbit crowed. "You'd chip every one, just like last time."

"Wait," Sweetflag cried, as Henbit turned to go back inside. "I'll do all the mending. I know how to sew, from watching you guys. It can't be that hard, right?"

Turning back to Sweetflag, Henbit crossed her arms. "And since when can you thread a needle?"

Cloudberry was gazing at the roly poly on the rock. "Why don't you like them, Hennie? Roly polies, I mean. It's not like they bite or anything."

"I like them fine. Now, if you'll both excuse me, I've got work to do."

"So you're not scared?" Sweetflag called after her sister.

"Certainly not," Henbit huffed, disappearing into the dark tunnel which led back to her room.

"Think of it Hennie, all the mending for a week. Two weeks. A month!" Sweetflag sang out.

"Flag, you really do need a spanking," Cloudberry said as Henbit reappeared.

"Me, pick up a roly poly, and Flag, do all the mending for a month," Henbit pondered. She glared at Sweetflag. "And no sneaking off or funny business like last time?"

"Sprout's honor."

"All right, then. You've got yourself a deal."

"You don't have to do this," Cloudberry whispered.

Henbit gritted her teeth. "Like you said, it's just a roly poly." Trying not to flinch, she forced herself to look down at the little creature. It truly was hideous. She clamped one eye shut and knelt down. She gave its hard, ridged back the briefest of touches before jerking her hand away. She shuddered as the roly poly contracted into a tight, hard ball.

Henbit shuddered as the roly poly contracted into a tight, hard ball.

"There. I did it!" She rose breathlessly.

"But the deal was to pick it up," Sweetflag reminded her.

Henbit threw Cloudberry a look of misery. Her face puckering as if she might cry, she bent down a second time. Her hand quivered as she let out a breath that was part sigh, part sob. With another deep shudder, she reached out and picked up the roly poly.

"Ugh," she cried; the roly poly filled half of her small frendible's hand. Recoiling violently, she shook the creature from her.

"There! Are you satisfied? I did it! I picked up the stupid thing."

Bursting into tears, Henbit hurried back to her room, not to reappear that afternoon.

CHAPTER 3

Toward evening, Cloudberry tiptoed into Henbit's room. The basket of mending had been set by the doorway for Sweetflag. Henbit was lying on the bed, her tear-swollen eyes covered with a damp towel.

"Hennie? Isn't it time to be starting dinner?" Cloudberry whispered.

"You'll have to manage without me tonight," Henbit mumbled.

"Oh. Well, all right. I suppose we can... forage or something. I really just came in to check on you, see how you were doing. That was an ugly trick Flag pulled."

Henbit took the cloth from her eyes and stared up at the earthen ceiling. "Did you see me touch it, Cloudy? Did you see me pick it up even though it made me sick? I showed her, didn't I? And now she's got to do all the mending for a month."

Cloudberry sat down on the bed beside her sister. "Yep, you showed her, all right. She's already asked me how to find the end of the thread on the spool. She's starting to look a little worried."

Henbit sat up and smoothed back her damp auburn hair. "She's out of control, Cloudy. Somebody's got to teach her a lesson. A lesson she'll never forget. Somebody's got to show her!"

"Now, Hennie, we must be tolerant. She is our sister, after all. Maybe it's just a phase."

"A phase!" Henbit pounded the mattress with her fist. "Flag has been going through this phase since the day she sprouted. She's got to change, Cloudy, and I'm telling you she's not going to unless somebody makes her!"

"You don't really mean that," Cloudberry soothed.

"Oh, don't I?" Henbit glowered.

The next afternoon was cold and rainy. Henbit had recovered from her roly poly ordeal, and was in her room filing recipe cards into a little box. Suddenly, Cloudberry burst sobbing through the doorway. Her hands clutched a crumpled blouse.

"Cloudberry, what's happened? Is everything all right?" Henbit exclaimed.

Cloudberry's hands trembled as she thrust the blouse at Henbit. "You see what she did?" she cried. "First, she took my best blouse without asking. Then she spilled grape juice all over it. And then she hid it under her bed! It's ruined!"

Cloudberry mopped her tears with the stained fabric. "You sewed this blouse for me, Henbit, and it took me weeks to embroider. Weeks! Flag knew that."

Henbit turned to file another card into the box. "So, what was that you were saying about 'phases'?"

Cloudberry stopped crying and stared at her sister. "And what were you saying about teaching somebody a lesson?"

"It took me weeks to embroider this!"

CHAPTER 4

That night the rain ended. The following day was clear and a little warmer. Henbit and Cloud-berry went outside where they found Sweetflag sitting cross-legged at the base of her favorite tall pine. She was whittling a piece of wood with a small knife.

Underneath her sweater, she wore the same soiled T-shirt and shorts as the previous two days. Her bangs remained untrimmed despite her earlier promise to Henbit. She saw her sisters and held up her handiwork.

"Fishing hook," she reported.

"Oh, for your fishing trip next week," Henbit said with a smile. "How talented of you, Flag. I hope you catch us lots of minnows."

Cloudberry was smiling, too. "Flag, you really are quite versatile. I peeked in your room earlier and saw that you've already tackled that mending. Super job, keep up the good work!"

Sweetflag threw both sisters a suspicious glance. "No problem," she said.

"You know, I really have been meaning to thank you," Henbit went on pleasantly. "In challenging me to pick up that roly poly the other day, you helped me to face one of my deepest, darkest fears." She gave a merry laugh. "Roly polies. What a silly thing to be afraid of."

"I thought so, too." Sweetflag agreed.

Henbit colored. "Yes, well, I... anyway, because of you, I've not only conquered my fear, but can sense I'm on the verge of doing things I never dreamed possible. I can feel myself becoming more spontaneous and adventurous by the minute, Flag – just like you!"

Sweetflag set down her work and peered from one sister's face into the other. "What are you two up to?" she demanded.

"Why, it's simple," Cloudberry told her. "Henbit's got a new wager for you."

"That's right," Henbit said. "If I can climb to the top of that dogwood tree over there... well, I would never force you to pick up a roly poly or anything like that... but I WOULD make you EAT a great big bowl of them!"

"Not raw, of course. Stewed," Cloudberry clarified.

"Are you crazy?" Sweetflag's face contorted as she considered the wager. "And what if Henbit can't make it up the dogwood?"

"Then SHE will consume the bowl of stewed roly polies."

"But she's never climbed a tree in her life. She's afraid of heights. She doesn't have any muscles."

Henbit looked hurt, but countered, "If it will prove I'm serious, why don't we set the date for next week? Maybe the day after your fishing trip. That way, I'll have time to get myself in the best possible shape before the climb. I'm tired of being boring, Flag. I want to be adventurous and fun – like you!"

"If that's true, then why that puny little dog-wood? Why not this tall pine here? That's the one I like to climb." Sweetflag patted the rough bark behind her.

"I said I wanted to be adventurous and fun, not dead," Henbit retorted. "You know as well as I do that I could never make it up one of the taller trees, no matter how hard I tried. No, the smaller dogwood will be plenty challenging. But I say I can do it!"

Sweetflag stood up and grinned. "And I say you can't."

"Does that mean you're in?" Cloudberry asked, her excitement building.

Sweetflag started to giggle. "It sure does. Just think of it, Hennie. A nice big bowl of stewed roly polies, just for you. All steaming and mushy and slimy and crunchy... Bet you can't wait!"

CHAPTER 5

The days went by slowly, but the morning of Sweetflag's fishing trip arrived at last.

"Bog Bilberry! Pokeweed! You can come out now, she's gone!" Henbit and Cloudberry called out. Two male frendibles emerged from the tunnel.

"Which tree did you want our help with?" Bog Bilberry asked, looking around at the many towering pines.

"That one." Henbit pointed to a small, spindly dogwood nestled among them.

"You're very nice to help us out," Cloudberry added.

Bog Bilberry chuckled. "Why, it's no trouble at all."

Bog Bilberry chuckled. "Why, it's no trouble at all. That Flag's had it coming for a long time now, ain't she, Poke? She dulls my best blades and don't sharpen them back."

"And she goes and gets my ropes all jumbled up," Pokeweed agreed. "Not to mention the way she does you two," he added, giving the sisters a nod.

The two friends got to work with their axes. By mid-afternoon, the job was finished and the small tree lay on its side. They laid down their tools and went inside for a short nap before supper.

It was nearly evening when Sweetflag trudged into the clearing, her bucket filled nearly to the top with minnows. Even though she was very tired, she noticed the felled dogwood tree at once, as well as the two axes laying on the ground beside it.

"Hey! Who cut down the dogwood tree?" she demanded. "I thought that was the one Hennie was going to climb tomorrow."

"It is," Henbit said, looking smug.

"And she is going to climb it, right to the very top. Aren't you, Hennie?" Cloudberry said.

Sweetflag threw down her fishing pole and tackle. "But that's cheating," she shouted. "That tree is laying on its side, for crying out loud. The top is practically touching the ground!"

"I don't recall your saying it had to be standing in order for me to climb it," Henbit replied coolly.

"It never occurred to me you'd have it chopped down first! Of all the sneaky, rotten tricks! Hey, Bog! Poke! Get out here, I know you're behind this. And you, Cloudy – guess what? She still won't be able to climb it. She'll still fall off, because guess what? She's just a big puffy prissy pants who thinks she knows everything! Why can't you both just stay inside like you're supposed to and mend and file cards and, and DUST!"

Sweetflag snatched a fistful of minnows from her bucket and hurled it at her sisters. She stormed to her room where the others could hear her muffled voice, yelling.

CHAPTER 6

The next morning after breakfast, everyone gathered around Henbit and the downed dogwood tree. Henbit was wearing a faded pair of overalls and Old Verbena's gardening gloves. Her curly auburn locks were tucked into a kerchief. Sweetflag, the last to appear, stood looking on sullenly.

"All ready? And, she's off!" Bog shouted.

With a tortured grunt, Henbit hoisted herself onto the base of the tree. Hugging the rough trunk with her elbows, knees and face, she began to inch her body forward. Her climb took far longer than even Cloudberry expected, but after an hour of concentrated effort, she reached the tip.

Henbit hoisted herself onto the base of the tree.

"Hennie, you did it, you didn't fall off!" Cloudberry cried, clapping her hands.

"There," Henbit gasped, half jumping, half falling to the ground. Even though the morning was chilly, the young frendible was drenched in sweat and her arms and legs were trembling. She staggered to Bog Bilberry, who offered his arm.

"Hooray for Henbit," Cloudberry and Pokeweed cheered. "Henbit wins the bet!"

Her bangs still covering most of her eyes, Sweetflag stood apart from the group with her arms crossed, scowling.

"Yeah, well. I guess you showed me, didn't you?"

Henbit looked into Sweetflag's unhappy face, and felt a stab of remorse. "Oh, Flag, I'd never force you to eat a bowl of roly polies or anything as awful as that. I was just trying to teach you a lesson. It was mean of you to dare me to pick up something I was so afraid of."

"And mean to take my favorite blouse without asking and then ruin it," Cloudberry broke in.

"And hey, stop messing up my knife blades already," Pokeweed added.

Drawing herself up, Sweetflag said, "Well, it just so happens that I love roly polies – stewed, fried or raw. I eat them all the time, as a matter of fact. So. Where's lunch? I'm starving."

Bog Bilberry grimaced. "Your 'lunch' is right over there, missy, on that rock. Henbit wasn't up to it, so I picked and cooked them roly polies myself. Looked under every rock in the forest, I did."

"But it was all in the heat of the moment," Cloudberry explained. "Nobody expects you to actually eat them."

"Hmph," Sweetflag replied. She strode to the rock, sat down, and tucked in the napkin Henbit had placed beside the full, steaming bowl.

No one could bear to watch as Sweetflag began to eat the roly poly stew. But they knew that she was eating it, because when she got up a few minutes later, her face was green.

"Well," she said, removing the napkin and giving a big stretch. "It has been a rather long morning. After enjoying this extremely satisfying lunch, I believe I'll turn in for a little nap. Got a lot of mending to do this afternoon. See you later, everyone." Sweetflag walked, then ran into the tunnel, holding her stomach.

When Sweetflag got up a few minutes later, her face was green.

"We may have gone too far," Cloudberry whispered to Henbit.

"You may be right," Henbit agreed. "I'll go talk to her." She turned to follow her younger sister, but stumbled and fainted into Bog Bilberry's arms instead.

For Cloudberry, the day was a long one as she went back and forth from Henbit's room to Sweetflag's. Henbit was so sore that she was unable to move from her bed, and Sweetflag so sick that she could not stay in hers.

Cloudberry had not had as much experience as a nurse as Henbit, but at last she got both sisters off to a fretful sleep. She padded down the tunnel to her own room. Sinking into a chair, she picked up a piece of embroidery.

"Maybe now they'll learn to get along," she said to herself. Then she laughed. "Won't that be the day!"

In another minute Cloudberry, too, was fast asleep.

ABOUT THE AUTHOR

Marty Donnellan is a lifelong resident of Atlanta, GA, USA. She is a writer, doll maker, skater, grain growing enthusiast and founder/director of Joy Community Kitchen, Inc., a 501(c)3 non-profit food charity. She is the author of six books – four set in the fictional world of frendibles, and two "how-to" manuals, one teaching doll making and the other, roller skating!

www.ingramcontent.com/pod-product-compliance
Lightning Source LLC
Chambersburg PA
CBHW071228130626
46555CB00004B/1890